COLLEGE FOOTBALL CHAMPIONSHIP

ALL-TIME GREATS

BY ANTHONY STREETER

Book design by Jake Slavik
Cover design by Jake Slavik

Photographs ©: Gerald Herbert/AP Images, cover (top), 1 (top); Bill Nichols/AP Images, cover (bottom), 1 (bottom); Eric Draper/AP Images, 4; Brian Bahr/Allsport/Getty Images Sport/Getty Images, 7; Ted S. Warren/AP Images, 8; Mitchell Layton/Getty Images Sport/Getty Images, 10; Mark Humphrey/AP Images, 13; Kevin C. Cox/Getty Images Sport/Getty Images, 15; Don Juan Moore/Getty Images Sport/Getty Images, 16; Ezra Shaw/Getty Images Sport/Getty Images, 18; Jonathan Bachman/Getty Images Sport/Getty Images, 20

Press Box Books, an imprint of Press Room Editions.

ISBN
978-1-63494-861-6 (library bound)
978-1-63494-879-1 (paperback)
978-1-63494-914-9 (epub)
978-1-63494-897-5 (hosted ebook)

Library of Congress Control Number: 2023923048

Distributed by North Star Editions, Inc.
2297 Waters Drive
Mendota Heights, MN 55120
www.northstareditions.com

Printed in the United States of America
082024

ABOUT THE AUTHOR

Anthony Streeter is a former sportswriter who has written for various newspapers. He lives in Columbia, Missouri, with his wife and three kids.

TABLE OF CONTENTS

PRICE
37

CHAPTER 1

TRUE CHAMPIONS

The first college football game was played in 1869. But for most of the sport's history, teams didn't compete in a national title game. Instead, sportswriters or coaches voted for which team they thought was the best.

In 1998, the Bowl Championship Series (BCS) changed that. Under this system, the top

STAT SPOTLIGHT

BCS CHAMPIONSHIP GAME RECORD

LONGEST TOUCHDOWN CATCH

Peerless Price: 79 yards (1998)

two teams would play each other. In the first championship game, Tennessee wide receiver **Peerless Price** stole the show. He recorded only four catches. But they went for 199 yards and a touchdown. Price's performance helped the Volunteers beat Florida State 23–16.

Florida State played in the first three BCS title games. Wide receiver **Peter Warrick** practically won the 1999 championship by himself. He caught six passes for 163 yards and two touchdowns. He scored another touchdown on a 59-yard punt return. He even caught a two-point conversion. Warrick led his team to a 46–29 win against Virginia Tech.

Offenses often shine in the title game. But in 2000, defense was on full display. **Torrance Marshall** led a tough Oklahoma Sooners defense. The linebacker

had six tackles and an interception in a 13–2 win against Florida State.

Offense came back the next year. Nebraska couldn't do much to stop Miami in 2001. Wide receiver **Andre Johnson** began the rout with

CLARETT
13

a 49-yard touchdown catch. Miami led 34–0 at the half. The Hurricanes eventually won 37–14. Johnson's two touchdowns and 199 receiving yards were a big reason why.

Miami was loaded with talent. Many fans expected the Hurricanes to win again in 2002. Instead, Ohio State pulled off an upset. Buckeyes freshman running back **Maurice Clarett** had been a force all season. In double overtime, he ran into the end zone for a 5-yard score. That touchdown proved to be the winner. For the first time in more than 30 years, Ohio State was the national champion.

SPLIT CHAMPIONS

The BCS wasn't a perfect system. In 2003, three teams ended the regular season with one loss. Defensive lineman Marcus Spears and Louisiana State (LSU) shut down Oklahoma for the BCS title. But Southern Cal (USC) also won its bowl game. So LSU was the BCS champ. But the sportswriters picked USC.

BUSH
5

CHAPTER 2

BCS SHINING STARS

The USC Trojans enjoyed a dominant 2003 season. However, the BCS picked two other teams for the title game. That motivated the Trojans. In 2004, USC quarterback **Matt Leinart** won the Heisman Trophy. This award is given to college football's best player each year. Leinart led the undefeated Trojans past Oklahoma for the BCS title.

The wins kept coming in 2005. USC running back **Reggie Bush** ran away from defenders all season. Voters awarded him the Heisman.

Leinart ranked third. But many thought runner-up **Vince Young** should have won. The Texas quarterback was big and fast with a strong throwing arm. Both Texas and USC ended the year undefeated. They met in a title game for the ages. Leinart put up big numbers. And Bush gained 279 total yards. But in the end, Young got his revenge. He scrambled for a late touchdown on fourth down to seal the win for Texas.

Tim Tebow shared the quarterback duties when Florida won the 2006 championship.

STAT SPOTLIGHT

BCS CHAMPIONSHIP GAME RECORD

TOTAL OFFENSE

Vince Young: 467 yards (2005)

TEBOW
15
ENGLISH
33
OKLAHOMA

Two years later, Florida was back in the championship game. The Gators ran 74 offensive plays in the 2008 title game. Thirty were Tebow passes. Another 22 were Tebow runs. The quarterback struggled early in the game. But his inspired play helped the Gators pull away. They beat Oklahoma 24–14.

Alabama claimed six national titles during the 1960s and 1970s. A new dynasty began in 2009. The Crimson Tide won three championships in four years. Elite defenses led the way. LSU didn't have a chance in the 2011 title game. Linebacker

CAM THE MAN

Cam Newton played just one season at Auburn. The dual-threat quarterback won the 2010 Heisman Trophy. Then he led the Tigers past Oregon for the BCS title. Newton battled injuries in the title game. Yet he still managed 329 all-purpose yards and two touchdowns in the win.

Courtney Upshaw racked up seven tackles and a sack in a 21-0 shutout. Linebacker **C. J. Mosley** was all over the field the next year. Alabama shut down Notre Dame 42-14.

Heisman winner **Jameis Winston** led Florida State back to the title game in 2013. It didn't start well for the quarterback. But Winston locked in when it mattered most. He led a late 80-yard drive. Winston threw a touchdown pass with only 13 seconds left. That clutch pass sealed a 34-31 comeback victory over Auburn.

ELLIOTT
15
2015

CHAPTER 3
PLAYOFF TIME

The BCS brought a championship game to college football. In 2014, the College Football Playoff (CFP) expanded the postseason to four teams. Ohio State and Oregon won their semifinals to reach the first CFP championship. In that game, Buckeyes running back **Ezekiel Elliott** couldn't be stopped. He tallied 246 rushing yards and four touchdowns. Elliott led Ohio State to a 42–20 win.

The next seven championship games featured either Alabama or Clemson. Three of them included both teams. Clemson couldn't

stop **Derrick Henry** in the 2015 title game. Alabama's punishing running back charged 50 yards for the opening touchdown. Then he kept on running and scoring in the 45–40 win.

Quarterback **Deshaun Watson** shined for Clemson in the loss. He and the Tigers got revenge against Alabama the next year. Watson racked up 463 yards of offense. His touchdown pass with one second remaining clinched the 35–31 win.

Clemson's **Trevor Lawrence** starred in the 2018 title game. The freshman quarterback was unfazed by Alabama's powerful defense. He coolly passed for 347 yards and three touchdowns. The performance helped the Tigers to a second championship in three years.

Joe Burrow wanted to be more than Ohio State's backup quarterback. So in 2018, he transferred to LSU for

BACKUP HERO

Freshman Tua Tagovailoa served as Alabama's backup quarterback in 2017. But with the Tide trailing Georgia 13–0 in the title game, he came off the bench. Tagovailoa led Alabama into overtime. Then he hit DeVonta Smith for a 41-yard touchdown pass to complete the comeback.

CHASE
1
LSU
2020
LSU
1

his junior season. It was the perfect fit. Burrow's crisp passes zipped to receivers **Ja'Marr Chase** and **Justin Jefferson**. Clemson had no hope of stopping LSU in the 2019 title game. In a record-breaking performance, Burrow threw for 463 yards and five touchdowns. He ran for another score. The undefeated Tigers won 42–25.

Quarterback **Stetson Bennett** arrived at Georgia as a walk-on. Eventually, he became the Bulldogs' starting quarterback. He left the school as a legend. Bennett led the team to championships in 2021 and 2022.

STAT SPOTLIGHT

CFP CHAMPIONSHIP GAME RECORD

RECEIVING YARDS

Ja'Marr Chase: 221 (2019)

TIMELINE

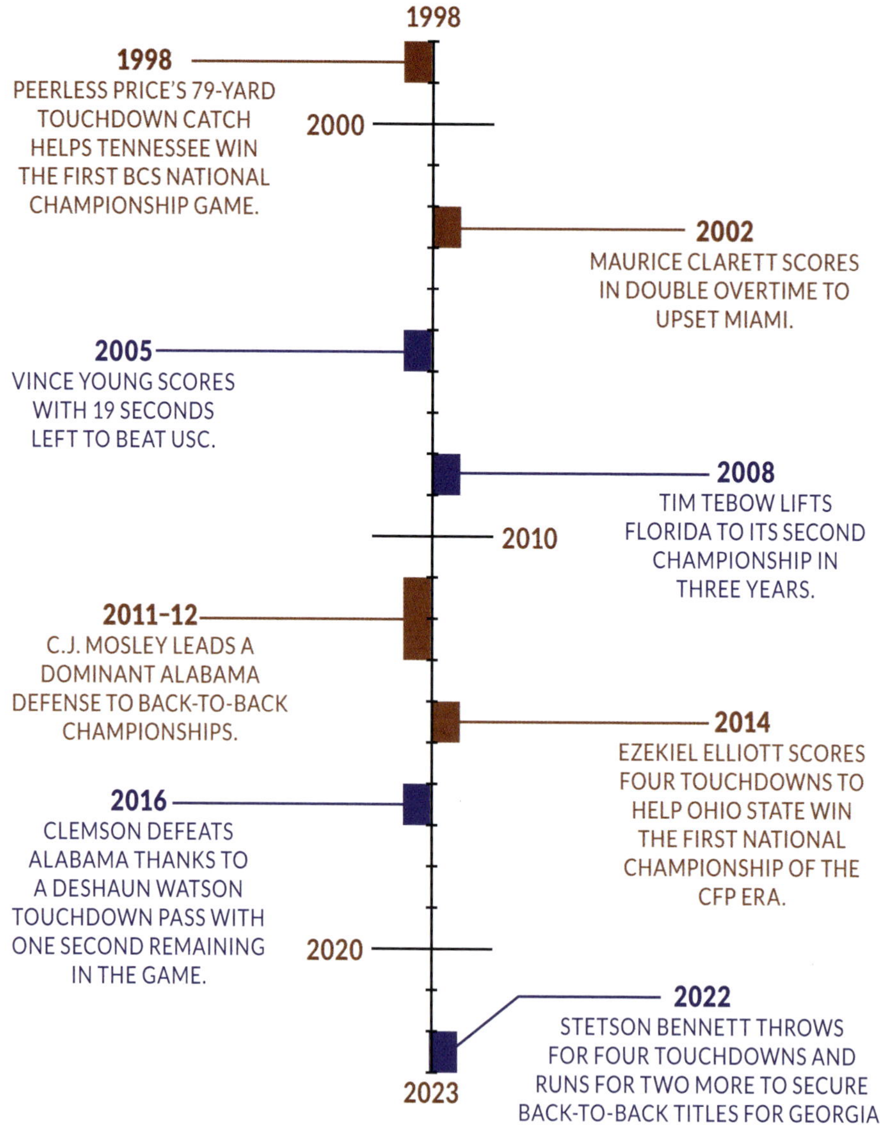

Timeline refers to the year in which the regular season took place. The national title game is held the following January.

CHAMPIONSHIP FACTS

COLLEGE FOOTBALL CHAMPIONSHIP

First played: January 4, 1999 (Bowl Championship Series), January 12, 2015 (College Football Playoff)

Most titles as a coach: Nick Saban, 7

Most titles by a team: Alabama, 6

Stats are accurate through the 2023 season.

MORE INFORMATION

To learn more about the College Football Championship, go to **pressboxbooks.com/AllAccess**.

These links are routinely monitored and updated to provide the most current information available.

GLOSSARY

all-purpose yards
Yards gained by passing the ball, running with the ball, and returning kicks, punts, or turnovers.

bowl game
A college football game that teams may be invited to play in after the regular season.

dual-threat
Good at both passing and running.

dynasty
A team that has an extended period of success, usually winning multiple championships in the process.

freshman
A first-year player.

overtime
An additional period of play to decide a game's winner.

rout
A game in which a team defeats its opponent easily.

scrambled
When a quarterback avoids defenders and gains yards by running the ball.

transferred
Switched from one school to another.

walk-on
A college athlete who had to try out for the team rather than being offered a scholarship.

INDEX